Arthur and the Pen-Pal Playoff

A Marc Brown Arthur GOOD SPORTS **Chapter Book**

Arthur and the Pen-Pal Playoff

Text by Stephen Krensky

Little, Brown and Company

Boston   New York   London

First Edition

Arthur® is a registered trademark of Marc Brown.

The characters and events portrayed in this book are fictitious. Any
similarity to real persons, living or dead, is coincidental and not intended
by the author.

Text has been reviewed and assigned a reading level by Laurel S. Ernst,
M.A., Teachers College, Columbia University, New York, New York;
reading specialist, Chappaqua, New York.

Library of Congress Cataloging-in-Publication Data

Krensky, Stephen.
    Arthur and the pen-pal playoff / text by Stephen Krensky. — 1st ed.
    p. cm. — (A Marc Brown Arthur good sports chapter book ; 6)
    Summary: After bragging to his pen pal about his basketball skills,
Arthur realizes that he has to make good on his boasts when the pen pal
comes to visit.
    ISBN 0-316-12054-5 (hc) / ISBN 0-316-12170-3 (pb)
    [1. Pen pals — Fiction. 2. Basketball — Fiction. 3. Aardvark — Fiction.
4. Animals — Fiction.] I. Title.

PZ7.K883 Arn 2001
[Fic] — dc21   2001037012

10 9 8 7 6 5 4 3 2 1

LAKE (hc)
COM-MO (pb)

Printed in the United States of America

For Shea Quadri

Chapter 1

* * * * * * * * * * *

"The pen is mightier than the sword."

Mr. Ratburn made this announcement to his third-grade class as he held out a pen and waved it in the air.

"Can anyone tell me what this means?" he went on. "Yes, Binky?"

"How big a pen are we talking about?"

Mr. Ratburn smiled. "Nothing out of the ordinary, I'm afraid. Just a regular pen. And a regular sword, too, I might add."

Binky frowned. He'd take his chances with the sword.

Fern raised her hand. "It means that

words and ideas are more powerful than just raw strength."

"Exactly," said Mr. Ratburn. "The words are from a play written by Edward Bulwer-Lytton. But for a pen to be mightier than a sword takes a great deal of practice. And all kinds of practice, too. So, today we'll be starting a new project — writing letters to students in another third-grade class on the other side of the state."

Everyone groaned.

"Now, now," said Mr. Ratburn, "think of this as an opportunity. This pen pal will know nothing about you. You will have the chance to present the very best impression of yourself. I've chosen your writing partners randomly. You can all start your letters for homework tonight."

At lunch everyone was talking about the assignment.

Buster was not pleased. "I hate writing letters," he said.

"How come?" asked Arthur.

"Well, for one thing, there's the writing part." He paused. "Actually, that's mostly it."

"The art of letter writing," said the Brain, "stretches back hundreds of years. People used to spend hours every day putting their thoughts together."

Fern sighed. "I had a friend from camp who sent poems to me. All her news rhymed, even the bad news."

"That would take me too long," said Muffy. "My grandmother and I do video conferencing. It's fast, it's easy, and she can see all my new clothes as soon as I get them."

"Well, I'm not going to discuss clothes with my pen pal," said Francine. "Her name is Laura Somebody. I can't remember. Anyway, I'm going to tell her my life story. That will keep her busy."

"I once wrote a letter to my cousin who

lives in Europe," said the Brain. "It took months and months to get an answer."

"Well, what did he say?" Francine asked.

"I don't know. He didn't write it in English."

"What about you, Arthur?" asked Francine. "What will you put in your letter?"

Arthur sighed. "I'm not sure. I don't want to bore my pen pal, but my life isn't very exciting. It would be much easier if I had once saved people from a burning building."

"You could write about the time I rescued that cat from the tree," said Buster.

"I don't think so," said Arthur. "But thanks for offering." He took a deep breath. "I'm sure I'll think of something."

Chapter 2

• • • • • • • • • • • •

Arthur sat at the desk in his bedroom and stared at the ceiling. He hadn't known before that there were very small cracks in one corner. But now he did and he had counted them all.

He turned back to the paper on his desk.

Dear Justin,

Hello. My name is Arthur. Arthur Read. This is my first letter to you. But I guess you know that since you've never gotten a letter from me before.

Arthur frowned at the paper. Then he crumpled it up and threw it in the wastebasket. How was he supposed to write a letter to someone he didn't know? What could he say that would be interesting? And what was interesting enough in his life to be worth telling a total stranger?

Arthur returned his gaze to the ceiling. Was that a new crack developing in the middle? Maybe he should keep an eye on it. It might get bigger and bigger, and pretty soon it —

Suddenly the door burst open. "Arthur, what are you doing?"

Arthur lowered his gaze to the doorway. "Go away, D.W.," he said. "I'm busy."

"You don't look busy. You were staring at the ceiling. Nobody doing that could be very busy."

"I'm thinking, D.W. I have homework to do."

"What kind of homework?"

Arthur sighed. "I have to write a letter to my pen pal. But I don't know him, and he doesn't know me, so I'm not sure what to say."

"If I had a pen pal, I wouldn't have any trouble writing about myself. Hey, that's an idea. If you think your life is too boring, you could write about your little sister. I could even tell you what to —"

"My life is not boring!" Arthur insisted. "It's just very regular. Reliable. Dependable. Other people wish their lives could be more like mine."

D.W. laughed. And then, before Arthur said anything else, she was gone.

"Good riddance," Arthur muttered. "Now I'll be able to concentrate."

Dear Justin,

I've been trying to write you a letter for a while, but every time I get started, my little sister comes in with a problem. She looks up to me so much that I hate to disappoint her. It's kind of a pain sometimes to be her hero, but I try to put up with it.

Arthur paused again. After a moment, he crumpled up this paper, too. Then he leaned back in his chair and fired the letter toward the wastebasket.

Swish!

"Nothing but net," said Arthur, as the paper settled to the bottom. He could hear his neighbors dribbling a basketball outside in their driveway. Arthur often joined in their games or played with his other friends.

He picked up his pencil and started to write.

Dear Justin,

Do you play basketball? We play a lot in our neighborhood. Whenever we choose teams, I'm picked first because of my fall-away jumper.

Arthur stopped for a moment and smiled at the paper. This was much better. Now he was finally getting somewhere.

Chapter 3

• • • • • • • • • • • •

"Over here, Arthur!"

Buster was waving to him from under the basket. They were playing in a three-on-three basketball game after school. Arthur, Buster, and Francine were on one team. The Brain, Binky, and Sue Ellen were on the other.

Arthur saw that Buster was open, but he couldn't break free of Sue Ellen. Finally, he looped a pass over her head — which the Brain intercepted. Buster came over to cover the Brain, but before he could reach him, the Brain fired up a jumper.

Swish.

Binky took the ball out with Buster guarding him. Binky tried to dribble down the line, but Buster reached in and knocked the ball out of bounds off Binky's hands.

"That's ours!" Buster shouted. "Take it in, Arthur."

Arthur slowly dribbled in from the backcourt. Sue Ellen was guarding him again. Arthur had to keep dribbling no matter what, because once he stopped, he wouldn't be able to start again — he'd have to pass or shoot.

He tried to fake Sue Ellen out — first to the left, then to the right. But Sue Ellen stuck with him. Finally, he fell back to take a shot. As his hands came up, she darted in and batted the ball away. Binky picked it up and drove in for an easy basket.

"That's the game," said Sue Ellen. "Want to play again?"

Arthur bent over, catching his breath.

"In a minute," he said.

"Nice move, Sue Ellen," said Binky. "You really had Arthur tied up in knots."

"I'm not tied up," Arthur insisted. "I just have a lot of things on my mind."

"Like what?" asked the Brain.

"Well, writing that letter to my pen pal, for one thing."

"I had a great time writing to mine," said Buster. "I told him all about my adventures as a detective. I wouldn't be surprised if he hired me for something."

"I wrote about my recent entry in the science fair," said the Brain. "Some people have given up on the idea of cold fusion as an energy source, but I still have hopes."

"I wrote about my big family reunion," said Francine. "I met cousins of cousins I didn't know existed." She turned to Binky. "What about your letter? Did you write it already?"

"Yup," said Binky.

"How did it turn out?" asked the Brain.

Binky thought for a moment. "Short," he said. "Very short."

"Mine was short, too," said Sue Ellen. "By the time I finished the fourth page —"

"The fourth page?" said Arthur. "You call that *short?*"

Sue Ellen shrugged. "I guess I didn't think I had much to say."

"So how much did you write, Arthur?" asked Francine.

"Um, I haven't finished yet."

"Mr. Ratburn wants all the letters turned in tomorrow," the Brain reminded him.

"No problem," Arthur insisted. "I'll have mine ready in the morning."

"Good," said Binky. "Then we still have time for another game if you can handle it."

"We can handle it," said Francine. "Right, Buster?"

He nodded. "Right. You ready, Arthur?"

"Ready," said Arthur, but he couldn't help sighing as he got up to play.

Chapter 4

• • • • • • • • • • •

The cafeteria was its usual busy place the following "Pizza Friday." All of the kids worked their way noisily through the line, choosing either cheese or pepperoni.

Arthur was near the end of the line. As he joined Francine, Binky, and the Brain at a table, Francine looked at him in surprise.

"Wow!" she cried. "How did you do that?"

"What do you mean?" asked Arthur.

"Look at your plate! You've got three slices of pepperoni!"

Arthur looked down. He hadn't really

been paying attention. Sure enough, Francine was right.

"Is that unusual?" he asked.

"Of course it is," she said. "I only got one. That's all anybody usually gets. You know how careful Mrs. MacGrady is."

"That's true," said Binky. "Once I saw two slices on my plate. But they only sat there for a second before she snatched one back."

"Not only that," said the Brain. "He's got six cubes of Jell-O. The rest of us only get four."

Everyone took a closer look.

"All right, Arthur, what's going on?" said Binky. "How come you're getting extra food?"

"I don't know, Binky. Honest. I didn't even talk to Mrs. MacGrady in line." He paused.

"What?" asked the Brain. "What do you remember?"

"Well, now that you mention it, Mrs. MacGrady did kind of smile at me a little."

"Did you say anything special to her?" asked Francine.

"No."

"Hmmmm," she said. "Very interesting. What do you think *that* means?"

Arthur had to admit he had no idea.

When they returned to the classroom, Mr. Ratburn was waiting for them.

"I have exciting news everyone," he said as they took their seats. "Remember those letters we wrote to that other class? Well, their replies were just delivered."

He handed them out one at a time.

"Keep in mind," he went on, "that every letter will be different. Just as each of yours reflected your interests and personality, theirs will do the same. I'll give you a few minutes to read and talk about them before we attack our math problems."

There was silence for a minute before anyone spoke.

"My pen pal has a skateboard," said Muffy. "She says here that she fell off a lot at the beginning, but not so much anymore."

"Mine likes fossils," said Francine. "His room is full of dinosaur skeletons."

"Mine says it was sunny when he wrote this," said Binky.

"What else did he say?" asked the Brain.

"Nothing. That was it. He kept it short." Binky beamed. "Hey, I like this guy."

"What about you, Arthur?" asked Buster.

"My pen pal seems to be really good at basketball," Arthur said slowly. "And, um, he's really glad that I am, too."

Francine laughed. "No offense, Arthur, but where would he get that idea?"

"From me, I'm afraid," said Arthur.

Chapter 5

. . . .

After school, Arthur got the chance to explain what had happened. He met with his friends out by the bike rack.

"I wasn't exactly bragging," he said to Buster, the Brain, Sue Ellen, and Francine. "I mean, it would be bragging if I were really good at basketball."

Francine frowned. "But then why write about basketball at all?"

"I was stuck. No matter what part of my life I thought about, it didn't seem interesting. I could hear someone playing basketball outside, so it just put the idea in my head. The basketball stuff just sort of took over."

"Just how good did you make yourself?" asked the Brain.

Arthur turned red. "Well, I kind of got into it, talking about dribbling with either hand and making blind passes over my shoulder."

"Oh, well," said Buster. "Look on the bright side. It's not like you'll ever have to prove how good you are. I mean, this kid lives on the other side of the state."

"ARTHUR!"

Mrs. MacGrady was calling to him from the cafeteria door.

"Could I speak to you for a minute, please?"

Arthur shrugged to the others and went over to talk to her. They watched from a distance.

"Something strange is happening," Francine observed.

"What do you mean?" asked Buster,

"The more Mrs. MacGrady talks, the shorter Arthur is getting."

"He's not getting shorter," said the Brain. "He's just slumping."

"Well, he sure looks shorter."

When Arthur made his way back to them a few minutes later, he looked like he was moving in slow motion.

"You won't believe it," he muttered.

"What?" they all said together.

"Justin is Mrs. MacGrady's grandson. I guess she's the one who suggested to Mr. Ratburn that Justin's class exchange letters with ours. And she says that Justin really liked my letter."

"That's not so bad," said the Brain. "And it explains why you're getting special treatment at lunch."

"There's more," said Arthur. "Justin is coming to visit over the weekend. And Mrs. MacGrady wants us to get together."

He shook his head. "I can't believe it. A whole class full of kids and I had to get the one whose grandmother lives here. What are the chances of this happening?"

"Actually," said the Brain, "the odds of such things happening are not what you expect. It turns out that —"

"BRAIN!"

He cleared his throat. "Small, very small, subatomic, really."

Arthur sighed. "Okay, okay. The bigger question is, what am I going to do?"

"Do?" Buster frowned. "Why do you have to do anything?"

"Because Justin wants to play basketball with me. A two-man playoff, Mrs. Mac-Grady called it."

"When is this going to happen?" asked the Brain.

"Over the holiday weekend."

"Maybe you're going away," Buster suggested.

Arthur shook his head. "We're not."

"Maybe you could just pretend to be busy."

"Oh, sure. You didn't see the smile on Mrs. MacGrady's face. She's looking forward to this. If I back out, who knows what I'll find in my lunches from now on." He shook his head. "I'm doomed, that's all. Doomed, doomed, doomed."

Chapter 6

• • • • • • • • • • • •

"Arthur, you're not eating," said his mother.

The family was sitting around the dinner table. While D.W. and Kate had almost cleared their plates, Arthur's looked almost untouched.

"I hope this doesn't mean a thumbs-down on the stuffed green beans," said his father.

"No, no," said Arthur, hurriedly taking a bite.

"The secret," his father went on, "is not cooking the beans for too long. This way they stay crunchy."

"These are very crunchy," said D.W.

Mr. Read smiled. "I think they could start a trend in appetizers. Crunchy — with a surprise inside. That's how I'll market them."

"Speaking of swallowing," said Arthur, "have you read anything lately about a pill you can take to make you really good at something overnight?"

His mother gave him a look. "Arthur, are you having trouble with your homework?"

"Oh, no, it's not that. I was just wondering . . ."

"I always wanted a pill like that when I was studying French," said his father. "Eat it with dinner on the plane to Europe, and . . . presto! When you got there, you'd be able to speak and read everything." He sighed. "I used to think a lot about those pills at test time." He looked at Arthur. "You have any tests coming up?"

"Not in school," Arthur said truthfully. "I was just curious."

After dinner, Arthur headed quickly up to his room. A pill! How could he have said something so silly? It just showed how desperate he felt. Maybe there were some books he could read from the library. Maybe he could practice in his head. Or what if . . .

The door to his bedroom burst open.

"I know what's really going on," said D.W.

Arthur stopped short. "You do?"

She nodded. "You don't fool me, you know."

"I don't?"

"Nope. You're my brother, Arthur. I know how you think."

"D.W., I really don't have time —"

"This is about school, isn't it?"

Arthur paused. "What do you mean?" he asked.

"I can tell. You've got that school look on your face."

"Don't be silly, D.W. You're just —"

The phone rang.

"I'll get it!" Arthur called out. "Sorry, D.W., can't talk now."

He ran into his parents' bedroom.

Arthur picked up the phone. "Hello?"

"Hi, Arthur," said the Brain. "I've been thinking about your, um, situation."

"So have I."

"Oh," said the Brain. "Have you come up with a plan?"

"Is running away to join the circus a plan?"

The Brain was silent for a moment. "I don't think so. It would seem then that we have only one choice."

"What's that?"

"We're just going to have to make you a better basketball player."

"Really?" said Arthur. "You think we can do that?"

There was another long pause. "Well," said the Brain finally, "we can certainly give it a try."

Chapter 7

· · · · · · · · · · ·

When Arthur arrived at the park Saturday morning, he found the Brain waiting for him.

"You're late," said the Brain.

"I am?" said Arthur.

The Brain looked at his watch. "Two minutes." He held out his arm. "See for yourself."

"No, no," said Arthur, "I believe you. I just didn't know it mattered."

The Brain blew the whistle that was hanging around his neck. "If we're going to take this seriously," he said, "everything matters."

Arthur nodded and straightened up. "Okay," he said. "And I want you to know, Brain, I really appreciate your doing this. I'm glad it's just the two of us, though, because —"

"Hi, guys!" shouted Francine.

She and Buster waved as they rode up on their bicycles.

"Um, hi," said Arthur, feeling a little embarrassed. "What brings you two —"

"I hope we're not late," said Sue Ellen and Binky, jogging up from behind them. "Binky had trouble keeping up."

"Did not!"

"Did, too."

Arthur looked at the Brain. "I thought we were going to do this ourselves."

"So did I," said the Brain. "At least at first. But then I asked Francine for some advice, and before I knew it, everyone was involved."

"We don't want some kid from another

town making you look bad," said Francine.

"That's right," said Binky. "If anyone's going to make you look bad, it's going to be us."

"Anyway," said the Brain, "since we're all here, let's get started. Now, Arthur, basketball is a game of parts. None of us is good at all of them — we each have our specialty. For Francine it's dribbling. Binky has rebounding, Sue Ellen relies on her jump shot, Buster has positioning, and I have general conditioning."

"General conditioning?" asked Arthur.

"That's where you run around and sweat a lot," Binky explained.

Arthur started to feel a little dizzy — and he hadn't done anything yet.

"Think of us as Team Arthur," said Buster. "We won't give up if you won't."

For the next hour, they put Arthur through a series of drills.

"Not that way, Arthur. Keep your eye on your opponent, not the ball," said the Brain.

"Faster, Arthur," said Francine. "And try not to trip over your own feet so much."

"Don't shoot from your chest. Get your arms higher," Binky said.

Arthur finally called for a time-out.

"You're not tired, are you?" asked Binky.

"Yes . . . I'm . . . tired," said Arthur, panting. "You guys are taking turns, but I'm in every play."

"All right," said the Brain. "You can rest for a minute. We can turn our attention to strategy. Since it's just you and him, that simplifies matters."

"It does?"

"Sure. We don't have to worry about a zone defense versus man-to-man. And you can't be double-teamed playing against only one other person."

The others continued speaking, but after a couple of minutes, Arthur stopped hearing the words. He could see his friends moving their lips, but his brain refused to take any more in.

"Are you listening?" asked Francine. "Your eyes have that spacey look."

"Earth to Arthur," said Buster. "Come in, Arthur."

Arthur sighed. "I'm here, Buster. But I can only learn so much at once. I don't suppose you think I've improved enough already."

Nobody spoke.

"It's hopeless," said Arthur. "I'm hopeless. When Justin takes the court, I'm sunk."

"No, you're not," said Buster. "I'm sure you'll be just fine."

But he didn't sound very convincing.

Chapter 8

· · · · · · · · · · · ·

When Arthur got home, every part of his body was sore. He had heard once that the human body has 206 bones. Right now he felt very sure that each and every one of them was trying to get his attention.

D.W. was reading a book on the living room couch when he came in. "You look terrible," she said.

Arthur sighed. "Thanks, D.W."

"I mean it, Arthur. Are you sick or something?"

Arthur paused to think about this. Maybe he was sick. And not just ordinary sick, either. Mrs. MacGrady couldn't be

41

mad at him for being sick, especially if it clearly wasn't his fault.

Arthur lay in the hospital bed staring at the doctors gathered around him.

"I've never seen a case like this," said the first doctor, stroking his chin.

"It's not like anything in the textbooks," said the second doctor.

The third doctor scratched his head. "I remember once hearing about a similar case in South America. It was in a remote village thousands of miles up the Amazon. Some kind of rare poison, I think."

"Was it contagious?" asked the first doctor, taking a step back from the bed.

"Not that I recall. There was a polka-dotted snake involved somehow. It was all very mysterious."

"Did the patient recover?" asked the second doctor.

"Yes. But he was not allowed to play basketball for the longest time."

"So you're saying I shouldn't play basket-ball?" Arthur asked from the bed.

"I'm afraid not," said the first doctor. "You'll just have to be brave."

"I'll do my best," said Arthur.

"ARTHUR!"

Arthur blinked. "What is it, D.W.?"

"Didn't you hear me? Mrs. MacGrady's on the phone."

"The phone rang?"

"Yes, it rang. And I answered it because you were on some other planet."

"Did you tell her I was here?"

D.W. rolled her eyes. "Well, *yes*, because you are."

"All right, all right. Give me the phone."

She handed it to him.

"Hello . . . yes, Mrs. MacGrady, it's me. Oh, he is. Tomorrow morning . . . that's pretty soon, isn't it? . . . Yes, it certainly is exciting. I've been thinking a lot about meeting Justin, too. . . . Um, let me check."

Arthur put his hand over the phone. "D.W., think of some excuse I can use to be busy tomorrow."

His sister frowned. "Arthur, tomorrow's Sunday. Why would you be busy?"

"It just would have helped if . . . oh, never mind."

He uncovered the phone again. "Hi, Mrs. MacGrady. No, that was just my sister. I guess I'm free. . . . Good. I'll see you then. Bye."

Arthur hung up the phone. "Well, you were no help at all," he said.

D.W. looked confused. "Help? Help with what?"

"Saving my life, that's all," said Arthur, who realized that the ache in his bones was nothing compared to the sinking feeling that had taken over his stomach.

The game was really going to happen, and there was nothing he could do to stop it.

Chapter 9

· · · · · · · · · · ·

Arthur slowly put one foot in front of the other. Left . . . right . . . left . . . right . . . left . . . right. He felt like he was walking on Jupiter, where the gravity was so strong that taking even one step was a tremendous effort. But even so, Mrs. MacGrady's house was getting closer and closer.

Arthur tried to look on the bright side. At least he wasn't on center court in some big tournament. Of course, on a team he might have been able to get lost in the crowd. But here it was just one-on-one, and there was no place to hide.

When Mrs. MacGrady's house came into view, Arthur had a momentary thought to turn and run. But before he could act on it, he heard his name called.

"Arthur!"

Mrs. MacGrady had seen him from the window, and now she was waving to him from the front porch. So there was no escape.

"Arthur, I want you to meet my grandson, Justin."

She pulled on an arm behind her — and out came Justin.

"Um, hi," said Arthur.

"Right. Hi," said Justin.

Arthur tried to hide his surprise. Justin wasn't eight feet tall the way he had imagined. And he didn't have hands the size of oven mitts, which would have been perfect for dribbling or dunking the ball.

In fact, Arthur thought, *he looks a little like me.*

And the resemblance even extended to the nervous expression on Justin's face.

"Now, you boys go play your game," said Mrs. MacGrady, "and afterward we'll have cookies and lemonade."

"Oh, no!" said Arthur suddenly. He clasped his hands to his cheeks. "I forgot to bring my basketball."

Justin laughed. "That's funny because I forgot mine, too. But Grandma bought me a new one, special for the visit she said."

"Oh," said Arthur. "Very thoughtful of her."

Justin sighed. "Wasn't it? She's great, but sometimes she's . . . well, I mean, this whole game was her idea."

Arthur blinked. "Really?"

Justin nodded. "You know how grandmothers are. She'll be very disappointed if we don't play."

The moment of truth had come. Arthur

and Justin took up positions in the drive-way.

Arthur took the ball out first. He started to dribble, fully expecting Justin to steal the ball away at any moment. Strangely, Justin looked as tentative as he did.

Okay, said Arthur to himself. *Here goes . . .*

Arthur drove to the basket and threw up a shot. It clanged off the rim. Justin scrambled after the ball and took it out. He fired up a shot that sailed over the backboard out of bounds.

"The wind must have caught it," said Justin.

"I say that a lot myself," said Arthur, retrieving the ball from behind the bushes.

"You do? But I thought you never miss."

"Well . . ." Arthur paused. "The truth is, I exaggerated a little."

"You did?" Justin beamed. "That's great."

"Why? So now you can *really* clobber me?"

"No, no," said Justin. "You don't get it. You see, I exaggerated, too."

"You did?"

"Uh-huh!"

"So you're not exactly a star either?"

Justin shook his head. "Not even close."

Arthur smiled. "Then let's play."

Chapter 10

· · · · · · · · · · · · ·

An hour later, the Brain, Francine, and Buster rode up to Mrs. MacGrady's house on their bikes. Arthur and Justin were sitting on the porch eating cookies.

"I told you we were late," said Francine.

"Rats," said Buster. "We missed it."

"But it appears they both survived," the Brain noted.

"Hi, guys," said Arthur. "This is Justin. Justin, this is Francine, Buster, and the Brain."

"Okay," said Francine. "Enough with the introductions. How was the big game?"

"Yeah," said Buster. "Who won?"

"Won?" asked Arthur.

Arthur and Justin looked at each other.

"There was a game, wasn't there?" asked Buster.

Justin nodded. "There was a game, all right."

"I'm glad we've settled that," said Francine. "Now tell us what happened!"

"It was very exciting," said Arthur.

"A real cliff-hanger," Justin added. "Arthur played very well."

"Thanks, Justin. So did you."

"And . . . ," said the Brain.

"We want to know more," said Francine. "We want details."

"I may just write it up as a story," said Arthur. "It'll be great."

"Oh, come on, Arthur," said the Brain. "Don't leave us in suspense."

"Sorry," said Arthur. "You'll just have to wait."

"Well, what will you call it?" asked Buster.

Arthur smiled. *"Arthur and the Pen-Pal Playoff,"* he said.